Queen Ella's Feet

Level 3B

Written by Sally Grindley
Illustrated by Sandra Aguilar
Reading Consultant: Betty Franchi

About Phonics

Spoken English uses more than 40 speech sounds. Each sound is called a *phoneme*. Some phonemes relate to a single letter (d-o-g) and others to combinations of letters (sh-ar-p). When a phoneme is written down, it is called a *grapheme*. Teaching these sounds, matching them to their written form, and sounding out words for reading is the basis of phonics.

Early phonics instruction gives children the tools to sound out, blend, and say the words without having to rely on memory or guesswork. This instruction gives children the confidence and ability to read unfamiliar words, helping them progress toward independent reading.

About the Consultant

Betty Franchi is an American educator with
a Bachelor's Degree in Elementary and Middle
Education as well as a Master's Degree in Special
Education. Betty holds a National Boards for
Professional Teaching Standards certification.
Throughout her 24 years as a teacher, she has
studied and developed an expertise in Phonetic
Awareness and has implemented phonetic strategies,
teaching many young children to read, including
students with special needs.

Reading tips

 This book focuses on the *ee* sound.

Tricky and/or new words in this book

Any words in bold may have unusual spellings
or are new and have not yet been introduced.

> **Tricky and/or new words in this book**
>
> **my cold I to for her
> said the cart by you**

Extra ways to have fun with this book

After the readers have finished the story, ask them
questions about what they have just read.

*Why is the Queen unhappy at the beginning of the story?
Why does the maid look for a sheep?*

Make flashcards for each of the sounds within the
pronunciation guide. This will help reinforce letter/
sound matches.

I eat grass
in the day and
I read books
at night.

A Pronunciation Guide

This grid highlights the sounds used in the story and offers a guide on how to say them.

s as in sat	a as in ant	t as in tin	p as in pig	i as in ink
n as in net	c as in cat	e as in egg	h as in hen	r as in rat
m as in mug	d as in dog	g as in get	o as in ox	u as in up
l as in log	f as in fan	b as in bag	j as in jug	v as in van
w as in wet	z as in zip	y as in yet	k as in kit	qu as in quick
x as in box	ff as in off	ll as in ball	ss as in kiss	zz as in buzz
ck as in duck	pp as in puppy	nn as in bunny	rr as in arrow	gg as in egg
dd as in daddy	bb as in chubby	tt as in attic	sh as in shop	ch as in chip
th as in them	th as in the	ng as in sing	nk as in sunk	le as in bottle
ai as in rain	ee as in feet			

Be careful not to add an /uh/ sound to /s/, /t/, /p/, /c/, /h/, /r/, /m/, /d/, /g/, /l/, /f/ and /b/. For example, say /ff/ not /fuh/ and /sss/ not /suh/.

"**My** feet feel **cold**," weeps Queen Ella. "**I** need **to** keep my feet warm."

"Queen Ella needs a big sheet **for her** feet," **said** King Alex.

"I will seek a sheep," said Jen **the** maid.

Jen gets up in a **cart**.

"I need a sheep,"
Jen said to a bee.

"A sheep?" said the bee.
"I see a sheep **by** that tree."

"Queen Ella needs a sheep,"
said the bee to the sheep.

"Will I meet Queen Ella?"
asked the sheep.

"**You** will meet Queen Ella,"
said Jen.

"Queen Ella needs a sheep for her feet."

The sheep got in the cart.

"A sheep for Queen Ella's feet," said Jen to King Alex.

"A sheep?" said King Alex.
"But Queen Ella needs a sheet,
not a sheep!"

"I will keep the sheep for my feet!"
said Queen Ella.

OVER 48 TITLES IN SIX LEVELS
Betty Franchi recommends...

Some titles from Level 1

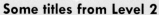

Bad Rat
978 1 84898 747 0

The Best Gift
978 1 84898 750 0

Clint and Grant Play I-Spy
978 1 84898 752 4

Bret and Grandma's Trip!
978 1 84898 751 7

Some titles from Level 2

Wish Fish
978 1 84898 755 5

Chuck and Duck
978 1 84898 756 2

Pink Bunny
978 1 84898 760 9

Let's go to the Swings
978 1 84898 759 3

Other titles to enjoy from Level 3

Bart's Go-Cart
978 1 84898 768 5

The Pop Duet
978 1 84898 767 8

Puff Flies
978 1 84898 765 4

An Hachette Company
First Published in the United States by TickTock, an imprint of Octopus Publishing Group.
www.octopusbooksusa.com

Copyright © Octopus Publishing Group Ltd 2013

Distributed in the US by
Hachette Book Group USA
237 Park Avenue, New York NY 10017, USA

Distributed in Canada by
Canadian Manda Group
165 Dufferin Street, Toronto, Ontario, Canada M6K 3H6

ISBN 978 1 84898 764 7

Printed and bound in China
10 9 8 7 6 5 4 3 2 1